MACBETH

SILVER EDITION

WILLIAM SHAKESPEARE

EDITED BY
ADAPTIVE READER

ISBN: 979-8-8692-9727-3

CONTENTS

Introduction   v

Dramatis Personæ   1

ACT I

SCENE I. An open Place   5
SCENE II. A Camp near Forres   7
SCENE III. A heath   10
SCENE IV. Forres. A Room in the Palace   17
SCENE V. Inverness. A Room in Macbeth's Castle   20
SCENE VI. The same. Before the Castle   24
SCENE VII. The same. A Lobby in the Castle   26

ACT II

SCENE I. Inverness. Court within the Castle   33
SCENE II. The same   37
SCENE III. The same   41
SCENE IV. The same. Without the Castle   48

ACT III

SCENE I. Forres. A Room in the Palace   53
SCENE II. The same. Another Room in the Palace   59
SCENE III. The same. A Park or Lawn, with a gate
leading to the Palace   62
SCENE IV. The same. A Room of state in the Palace   64
SCENE V. The heath   71
SCENE VI. Forres. A Room in the Palace   73

ACT IV

SCENE I. A dark Cave. In the middle, a Cauldron
Boiling   77
SCENE II. Fife. A Room in Macduff's Castle   84
SCENE III. England. Before the King's Palace   89

ACT V

SCENE I. Dunsinane. A Room in the Castle   101

SCENE II. The Country near Dunsinane   105

SCENE III. Dunsinane. A Room in the Castle   107

SCENE IV. The countryside near Dunsinane. A forest
in view.   111

SCENE V. Dunsinane. Within the castle.   113

SCENE VI. The same. A plain in front of the castle.   116

SCENE VII. The same. Another part of the plain.   117

Scene VIII. The same. Another part of the field.   120

INTRODUCTION

Welcome to Adaptive Reader, your portal to the captivating world of literature, tailored to fit your unique reading abilities.

In today's fast-paced and diverse learning environment, we believe in the power of personalized learning experiences. That's where the concept of leveled reading comes in, and why we, at Adaptive Reader, have dedicated ourselves to offering a broad collection of classic novels at various reading levels. Our mission is to make the joy and benefits of reading accessible to everyone.

THE BENEFITS OF LEVELED TEXTS

So, what exactly is leveled reading? It's an approach that matches students with texts that align with their unique reading abilities. This ensures that every reader is challenged just the right amount - enough to grow, but not so much that they feel overwhelmed or frustrated.

For students, this means you'll engage with texts that stretch your reading skills while keeping the experience enjoyable and manageable. You'll gain confidence as you successfully comprehend each level and feel motivated to explore more challenging texts as your reading skills grow.

For teachers, Adaptive Reader provides a valuable tool to support differentiated instruction. You can assign the same novel to your entire class while ensuring each student reads a version that aligns with their reading level. This allows all students to participate in class discussions and activities, fostering a more inclusive learning environment.

For parents, Adaptive Reader offers a supportive tool to encourage your children's reading journey. As your child progresses through the different levels of a novel, they'll not only enhance their reading skills but also develop a deeper love for literature.

READING ACROSS MULTIPLE EDITIONS

All of our leveled novels include passage markers that correspond to the same content across every one of our editions. This means that passage '62' in our silver edition contains the same themes and plot elements as passage '62' in our original edition.

For teachers, this means that you can say "let's look at passage 35 together. What is the author trying to tell us here?" and all of your students will be reading the same content — but with vocabulary and syntax that's adapted to their reading level.

Our online reading tool, available at www.adaptivereader.com, gives students and teachers free access to the original text with passage markers. We encourage teachers to include close readings of the original text as part of their coursework, giving all students exposure to the rich original syntax and language of these exceptional authors.

THE POWER OF LITERATURE

At Adaptive Reader, we are committed to helping everyone experience the power of literature. So whether you're a student diving into a classic novel, a teacher looking for flexible resources, or a parent seeking ways to support your child's literacy, Adaptive Reader is here for you.

We invite you to embark on this exciting literary journey with us. Enjoy the world of stories, characters, and ideas that await you in our collection of leveled novels. Happy reading!

DRAMATIS PERSONÆ

DUNCAN: King of Scotland.

MALCOLM: Duncan's Older Son.

DONALBAIN: Duncan's Younger Son.

MACBETH: Leader in the King's Army.

BANQUO: Another Leader in the King's Army.

MACDUFF: Important Man, or thane, from Scotland.

LENNOX: Important Man, or thane, from Scotland.

ROSS: Important Man, or thane, from Scotland.

MENTEITH: Important Man, or thane, from Scotland.

ANGUS: Important Man, or thane, from Scotland.

CAITHNESS: Important Man, or thane, from Scotland.

FLEANCE: Banquo's Son.

SIWARD: The leader of the English Army, and the Earl of a place called Northumberland.

YOUNG SIWARD: Siward's Son.

SEYTON: Macbeth's assistant.

BOY: Macduff's Young Son.

DOCTORS, an OLD MAN, SOLDIERS, LORDS, GENTLE-WOMAN, OFFICERS, MURDERERS.

LADY MACBETH: Macbeth's wife.

LADY MACDUFF: Macduff's wife.

HECATE and three WITCHES.

SCENE: In the end of the Fourth Act, in England through the rest of the Play, in Scotland, and chiefly at Macbeth's Castle.

ACT I

SCENE 1. AN OPEN PLACE

FIRST WITCH:
When will we three meet again?
In thunder, lightning, or in rain?

SECOND WITCH:
When the big fight is over,
When the battle is lost and won.

THIRD WITCH:
That will happen before the setting of the sun.

FIRST WITCH:
Where will it be?

SECOND WITCH:
On the open land.

THIRD WITCH:
There to meet with Macbeth.

FIRST WITCH:
I'm coming, Graymalkin!

SECOND WITCH:
Paddock is calling.
THIRD WITCH:
Soon.
ALL:
What's good is bad, and what's bad is good:
Hover through the foggy and dirty air.

They exit.

SCENE 11. A CAMP NEAR FORRES

[*Alarm sounds in the distance. Enter King Duncan, Malcolm, Donalbain, Lennox, with their helpers, who meet a wounded Captain.*]

DUNCAN:
Who is this injured man covered in blood?
It looks like he can tell us
About the current state of the rebellion.

MALCOLM:
This is the officer
Who bravely fought to prevent my capture.
Welcome, brave friend!
Tell the King what happened in the battle
As you left it.

SOLDIER:
It was an even fight.
It was like two tired swimmers holding onto each other
While fighting in the water. Everyone was tired.

The cruel Macdonwald had help
From other soldiers.
And Fortune, or Luck, seemed to favor him.
But that wasn't strong enough
Because brave Macbeth (he really deserves that title),
Ignored Fortune's favor and with his waving sword,
Found the traitor.
They never had a chance to shake hands, or say goodbye to him,
Until Macbeth slashed him from belly to chin,
And placed his head on our castle walls.
DUNCAN:
Oh courageous cousin! Perfect man!
SOLDIER:
Well, the sun can bring both thunder and comfort.
Pay attention, King of Scotland.
Justice had been served,
But everything changed quickly.
The Norwegian lord, spotting an advantage,
Suddenly brought in fresh troops and
Started a new attack.
DUNCAN:
Didn't this scare our leaders, Macbeth and Banquo?
SOLDIER:
Yes.
Just as sparrows fear eagles, or rabbits fear a lion.
However, I must say they were as charged as cannons!
They smacked the enemy with double strength.
But I am weak, my cuts need healing.
DUNCAN:
Yes. Your words and wounds show your honor.
—Quick, get him doctors.

       Exit Captain, attended. Enter Ross and Angus.

Who's coming now?
MALCOLM:

The noble Thane of Ross.
LENNOX:
He looks in such a hurry! That's how one should look
When they bring strange news.
ROSS:
God save the King!
DUNCAN:
From where do you come, noble thane?
ROSS:
From Fife, great King,
Where the Norwegian flags hang in the air.
Norway himself was helped by that unfaithful traitor,
The Thane of Cawdor.
Though the battle was terrifying,
The victory was ours.
DUNCAN.
Great joy!
ROSS:
And now,
Sweno, the King of Norway, asks for peace.
We wouldn't even allow to bury his soldiers.
We told him to give us ten thousand dollars
For our use at Saint Colme's Inch.
DUNCAN:
The Thane of Cawdor won't trick
Us anymore. Announce his immediate death,
And give Macbeth his old title.
ROSS:
I'll make sure it's done.
DUNCAN:
What the traitor has lost, the noble Macbeth has won.

Exit.

SCENE III. A HEATH

6   *[The sound of thunder brings the arrival of the three witches.]*

FIRST WITCH:

Where have you been, sister?

SECOND WITCH:

I've been killing pigs.

THIRD WITCH:

What about you, sister?

FIRST WITCH:

I met a sailor's wife who was eating chestnuts.

I asked her to share them, but she rudely refused.

Her husband has sailed to Aleppo on the ship called Tiger.

I'll sail after them and I'll get back at her.

SECOND WITCH:

I'll give you a gust of wind for your journey.

FIRST WITCH:

That's kind of you.

THIRD WITCH:

I'll give you another wind.

FIRST WITCH:

I've got all the other winds!

I'll bring him so much trouble that he'll wish he could sleep,

But sleep won't come either day or night.

He'll become weak and skinny after surviving hardship.

Even though his ship won't be lost, there'll be a big storm. See what I've got.

SECOND WITCH:

Show me, show me.

FIRST WITCH:

Look here, I have a pilot's thumb. It was destroyed as he journeyed home.

They hear a drum.

THIRD WITCH:

I hear a drum! Macbeth's coming.

ALL WITCHES:

We are witches of the sea and land.

We gather here three times for you and three times for me,

Then three more times for all of us, that makes nine.

Quiet, time to cast the spell.

Enter Macbeth and Banquo.

MACBETH:

I've never seen such a strange and confusing day.

BANQUO:

How far is it to Forres?—Who are these creatures,

So old-looking, dressed in such wild clothes,

They don't seem to belong to this earth,

But still, they're on it?—Are you alive? Or are you something

We can question? You appear to understand me,

But your fingers over your lips indicate that you're not willing to speak.

You look like women,

But your beards make me think otherwise.

MACBETH:
Speak, if you can;—who are you?
FIRST WITCH:
Everyone salute, Macbeth! Hello, Lord of Glamis!
SECOND WITCH:
Everyone salute, Macbeth! Hello, Lord of Cawdor!
THIRD WITCH:
Everyone salute, Macbeth! You will be king someday!
BANQUO:
Kind sir, why are you surprised and seem scared
by things that sound so good?—Honestly,
Are you imaginary, or are you really
What you appear to be? My noble friend
You greet warmly and predict much greatness
Including royal hope,
which has him entranced. Yet you don't speak to me.
If you can see into the future,
And tell which plans will work, and which will not,
Speak then to me, who neither begs nor fears
Your gifts or your hate.
FIRST WITCH:
Hail!
SECOND WITCH:
Hail!
THIRD WITCH:
Hail!
FIRST WITCH:
Less than Macbeth, and greater.
SECOND WITCH:
Not so fortunate, but much happier.
THIRD WITCH:
Your children will be kings, even if you are not:
So all salute, Macbeth and Banquo!
FIRST WITCH:

Banquo and Macbeth, everyone salute!

MACBETH:

Wait, you incomplete speakers, tell me more.

Since my father passed away, I know I am the Thane of Glamis,

But how am I now the Thane of Cawdor? The Thane of Cawdor is alive.

As for becoming a king,

That's an unbelievable thought too.

Where is this odd information coming from? Why do you

Stop us on this lonely and deserted moor,

With such unusual greetings? Speak up, I demand you.

Witches disappear.

BANQUO:

Just like there are bubbles in water,

These women were bubbles from the earth. Where did they disappear?

MACBETH:

Into thin air.

I wish they had stayed longer.

BANQUO:

Were those things real that we were just talking about?

Or did we eat something that's made us lose our senses?

MACBETH:

Your children will become kings.

BANQUO:

And you shall become a king.

MACBETH:

And the Thane of Cawdor too, is that not right?

BANQUO:

Exactly, that's what they said. Who's approaching now?

Ross and Angus enter.

ROSS:

The King is pleased to hear about your victory, Macbeth.

He was amazed to learn about

Your brave efforts during the fight with the rebels.
He is amazed and full of praise for you.
In fact, so many people brought
News of your bravery. They all spoke highly
Of your contributions to the kingdom's defense,
And showered him with news of your bravery.
ANGUS:
We've been sent
To thank you on behalf of our King.
Just to walk you into his presence,
Not to pay you.
ROSS:
The king also told me to call you the Thane of Cawdor.
That title belongs to you now.
BANQUO:
Wait, can the devil tell the truth?
MACBETH.
The Thane of Cawdor still lives. Why are you dressing me
In borrowed clothes? You're giving me a title that doesn't fit.
ANGUS:
Well, the one who was Thane is still alive,
But he is going to die.
He helped the rebels and brought disaster to his own country.
MACBETH:
[*Aside.*] Glamis, and Thane of Cawdor:
The greatest is still to come. [*To Ross and Angus.*]
Thanks for your efforts.
[*To Banquo.*] Don't you hope your children will be kings,
When those who gave me the Thane of Cawdor title
Promised no less to them?
BANQUO:
That, depending on how it's interpreted,
Might encourage you to seek the crown,
Besides the Thane of Cawdor. But it's odd--

And often to lead us to our downfall,
Forces of evil tell us partial truths.
They give us small honors, to later betray us
In very big and dangerous ways.
Cousins, could I have a word, please?

MACBETH.

[Aside.] Two truths have been told.
—I thank you, gentlemen.—
[Aside.] This supernatural suggestion
Can't be bad, but it also can't be good. If it's bad,
Why has it given me a taste of success,
Starting with the truth? I am now Thane of Cawdor.
If this is good, why does it lead to scary thoughts
That make my hairs stand on end,
And my heart pound in my chest? My real fears
Are less than my terrible thoughts.
My idea of murder is only in my mind.
Now I am confused and uncertain,
And nothing is but what it isn't.

BANQUO:

Look at how lost Macbeth is.

MACBETH:

[Quietly.] If luck will make me king, then, luck can crown me
Without any action from me.

BANQUO:

New titles are difficult for him.
Like a stranger's clothes, it does not yet fit,
And can only feel right once it's used.

MACBETH:

[Quietly.] Whatever will happen, will happen.
Time continues even during the toughest day.

BANQUO:

Noble Macbeth, we wait upon your wish.

MACBETH:

Bear with me. My slow mind was occupied
With forgotten matters. Kind gentlemen, your efforts
Are noted. Let's go toward the King.
Reflect on what has happened and when there's more time,
Having thought it over, let us share
What's on each other's minds.
BANQUO:
Very gladly.
MACBETH:
Until then, that's enough. Come, friends.

They exit.

SCENE IV. FORRES. A ROOM IN THE PALACE

11 *[MUSIC FLOURISHES. ENTER DUNCAN, MALCOLM, DONALBAIN, LENNOX, AND THEIR ASSISTANTS.]*

DUNCAN:
Has Thane of Cawdor been killed?

MALCOLM:
I spoke with someone who saw him die.
They said he admitted to what he had done
asked for your Highness' forgiveness. He died
as someone who accepted death and threw away
His like like it was nothing.

DUNCAN:
You really can't judge a book by its cover.
He was a man in whom I placed
My absolute trust.

Enter Macbeth, Banquo, Ross, and Angus.

Ah, my noble relative!

I owe you so much. Paying you back quickly still leaves me behind.

You deserve more than what anyone can repay.

MACBETH:

The service and loyalty I give is its own reward.

Like children and servants,

We do nothing more than what is expected.

We doing everything to ensure your love and honour.

DUNCAN:

Welcome here!

I have started to rely on you and will work...

To help you keep growing — Noble Banquo,

You also deserve praises, and everyone should know it.

Let me give you a hug

And keep you close to my heart.

BANQUO:

If I grow, the reward is all yours.

DUNCAN:

I am both happy and sad. What a day!

My sons, relatives, noblemen, and those close to me should know this.

Today we will give power to our oldest son, Malcolm.

We pronounce him from now on as the Prince of Cumberland, and heir to the throne.

Now, we'll head to Inverness, which will bring us even closer to Macbeth.

MACBETH.

The remaining work, not for my benefit, but yours.

I'll be the one to announce it, and fill my wife with joy

When I tell her of your coming;

So, I respectfully take my leave.

DUNCAN.

My trusted Cawdor!

MACBETH:

[*Aside.*] The Prince of Cumberland!—That position
Stands in my path! Stars, hide your light!
Don't let anyone see my dark, deep desires.
Even if the eye fears the hand's action, let it be.

Exit.

DUNCAN:
Right, noble Banquo! He is really courageous.
And when he's praised, I feel satisfied.
Such praise is a feast to me. Let's follow after him,
He's preparing a warm welcome for us.
He is truly a wonderful family member.

Exit. The sound of trumpets.

SCENE V. INVERNESS. A ROOM IN MACBETH'S CASTLE

13 *[LADY MACBETH ENTERS, READING A LETTER.]*

LADY MACBETH:

"The witches met me on victory day. I learned that they have more knowledge than a normal person. When I wanted to ask them more, they turned into thin air and vanished. While I was amazed by it all, I received messages from the King, who greeted me as 'Thane of Cawdor'—a title the witches had called me earlier. They also hinted at a future time when I would be king! I thought it would be good to tell you (my dearest partner in greatness) so you wouldn't miss out on the happiness that comes from knowing the greatness that is promised to you. Take this to heart and see you later."

You are Thane of Glamis and Thane of Cawdor.
And you will be what you have been promised.
But I'm worried about your kind nature.
You're so full of the milk of human kindness

That you'll miss the way to greatness.

You do want to be great, but you don't have the guts you need.

If you want to do something truly important,

You'll want to do it in an honest way.

You wouldn't cheat but yet you would wrongly become king.

You would listen to whoever says,

"This is how you must do it," to become king,

But you're afraid to get it done.

Yet you know it must be done.

Come to me, so I can fill your ears

With my plan and boost your courage with my words.

All that prevents you from reaching the crown,

Which destiny and supernatural help seem

To have prepared for your coronation.

Enter Messenger.

What news do you bring?

MESSENGER:

The King is coming here tonight.

LADY MACBETH:

You must be joking.

Isn't your boss with him? If that's so,

He would have informed us to get ready.

MESSENGER:

As you wish, it is true. Our thane is coming.

A messenger has informed us ahead of his arrival,

Who, nearly out of breath, could barely muster the energy

To deliver his message.

LADY MACBETH:

Take care of him.

He brings important news.

Messenger exits.

The raven's hoarse squawking signifies

The fatal arrival of Duncan

Underneath my castle's walls. Come, you spirits

That influence mortal thoughts, release me of my femininity here,
And fill me, from my head to my toes, completely
With the cruelest intentions! Thicken my blood,
And block my feelings of guilt,
So no natural feelings of remorse
Can interrupt my cruel plans, nor keep peace between
The deed and its effect! Come to my chest,
And turn my milk into bitter gall, you murdering helpers,
Wherever in your invisible forms
You cause nature's harm! Come, thick night,
And hide yourself in the darkest smoke of hell
So my sharp knife can't see the wound it creates,
Nor heaven glimpse through the darkness
To cry, "Stop, stop!"

Macbeth enters.

Great Glamis, deserving Cawdor!
Greater than both, by the title of king in the future!
Your letters have moved me beyond
The present reality, and I now feel
In a blink of an eye, we will be in the future.
MACBETH:
My dear love,
Duncan will be here tonight.
LADY MACBETH:
And when does he leave?
MACBETH:
He plans to leave tomorrow.
LADY MACBETH:
Oh, the sun will never shine on that morning!
Your showing all of your emotions on your face.
To fool everyone, pretend to be friendly and inviting.
Smile and welcome them warmly.

Act like an innocent flower, but be sneaky like a snake hiding underneath.

I will take responsibility for our actions tonight and in the future
And will have complete control and authority.

MACBETH:

We will talk more about this later.

LADY MACBETH:

Just remember to keep a clear face.
Making changes to your appearance can lead to suspicion.
Leave the rest to me.

Exit.

SCENE VI. THE SAME. BEFORE THE CASTLE

16 *[Enter Duncan, Malcolm, Donalbain, Banquo, Lennox, Macduff, Ross, Angus, and their attendants, with music playing. Macbeth's servants are waiting on them.]*

DUNCAN:

This castle is a pleasant place. The air
is quick and sweet, and it appeals
well to our senses.

BANQUO:

The martlet, a beloved bird of the summer, has made a nest here.
The air smells welcoming here. I've noticed, where this bird
chooses to build its nest and multiply,
The air is of high quality.

Enter Lady Macbeth.

DUNCAN:

Look, there's our honored hostess!—
Sometimes, the love people have for us can be a burden,
yet we are grateful for it. I am here to teach you

how you shall thank God for your hard work,
and let us thank you for the effort.
LADY MACBETH:
All of our service,
done enthusiastically and doubly so each time,
Is a simple task when compared to the great honors
you, Your Majesty, brings to our home: we trust and respect you.
DUNCAN:
Where's the Thane of Cawdor?
He rides well!
And his strong loyalty and love, as sharp as a spur, helped him
reach his home before us. Kind and noble hostess,
we are your guests tonight.
LADY MACBETH:
We are always at your service.
They have everything, themselves included, ready
To present when your Highness wants,
And will always return what is yours.
DUNCAN:
Give me your hand.
Guide me to my host. We appreciate him a lot,
And will keep showing our kindness towards him.
With your permission, hostess.

Exit.

SCENE VII. THE SAME. A LOBBY IN THE CASTLE

[THERE ARE MUSICIANS AND TORCHBEARERS. ENTER A LEAD SERVANT, FOLLOWED BY VARIOUS SERVANTS CARRYING TRAYS AND DINNERWARE. THEN ENTER MACBETH.]

MACBETH:

If this deed could be finished as soon as possible, it would be best.

If only carrying out this murder could lead directly to success!

If only this act could be the beginning and the end

—Here, right now.

But if not, we might risk our future lives.

Yet, when we rush into these types of situations,

Bad things can happen.

For example, if I do something awful, won't it come back to me?

This idea of equal punishment applies to us.

Here we are faced with bad deeds that are two times worse than anything.

First, because I am both his relative and subject,

I should not be committing the crime. And then, as his host,

I should be protecting him from harm, not planning to harm him myself.

Also, Duncan has been such a gentle and good king,

So honest in his role, that his goodness

Will shine like angels, speaking loudly against

The tragedy of his death.

People will drown out the wind with their tears.

—I don't have any really good reason to push me towards this dark plan,

Except for a desire for power, which tends to make people leap over the top,

And falls on the other side—.

Lady Macbeth enters.

Any news?

LADY MACBETH:

He's just about finished his meal. Why'd you leave the room?

MACBETH:

Did he ask for me?

LADY MACBETH:

Don't you know that he did?

MACBETH:

I don't want to proceed any further with this plan.

He's recently honored me, and I've earned

Praise from all sorts of people.

I want to enjoy it, not throw it all away.

LADY MACBETH:

Was your ambition a fantasy

That you told yourself? Has it faded since?

And does it wake up now, to look so worried and afraid

At what it so eagerly wanted? From now on

That's how I see your love. Are you scared

To act with the same boldness

That you desire? Would you prefer to have

What you consider the prize of life,
And live a coward in your own eyes,
Saying "I dare not" to your "I would,"
Just like the old tale about the scared cat?
MACBETH:
Hey, enough!
I dare to do what is fitting for a man.
Doing more than that is unnatural.
LADY MACBETH.
What kind of beast then,
Made you promise this undertaking to me?
When you were brave enough to do it, then you were a man.
And in order to be more than you were, you wanted
To be even braver. Neither time nor place
Were right then, and yet you wanted both.
Now that they have happened, they seem to unsettle you. I know
How sweet it is to love the baby who is nursing from me.
I would, even while it smiled up at me,
Have yanked myself from his toothless gums...
And I'd have done anything,
Even hurt a baby, had I made a promise like you
have made to me.
MACBETH:
What if we fail?
LADY MACBETH.
We fail?
Get your courage ready and we won't fail. When Duncan is asleep
(which he will be, from his long and tiring day), I'll offer his guards
Wine and get them into a heavy, drunken sleep.
Then, what can't you and I do to
The unprotected Duncan? We'll blame them.
MACBETH:

No daughters for you, just sons!
Your spirit would create nothing but boys.
So people will believe they did it?
LADY MACBETH:
Who would dare say otherwise?
After all, as we openly scream
Because of his death, how else will it look?
They will look guilty.
MACBETH:
I'm ready, and gearing up
Every part of me for this horrifying act.
Let's go, and pretend like nothing is wrong.
A fake face must hide what the disloyal heart knows.

Exit.

ACT II

SCENE 1. INVERNESS. COURT WITHIN THE CASTLE

[Banquo and Fleance enter, carrying a torch.]

BANQUO:
How is the night, son?
FLEANCE:
The moon has set. I haven't heard the clock.
BANQUO:
And it sets at twelve.
FLEANCE:
I think, it's later, dad.
BANQUO:
Here, hold my sword.—
The lights of the stars are all out. Hold this as well--
A hard task weighs heavily on me,
And yet I don't want to sleep. Kind powers,
Prevent these terrible thoughts in me that appear
When I'm at rest!

Enter Macbeth and a servant carrying a torch.

Hand me my sword.—Who's that?
MACBETH:
A friend.
BANQUO:
What, not in bed yet, sir? The king's asleep.
He had lots of fun and
Gave generous gifts to your helpers.
He sends this jewel to your wife,
Calling her a great hostess, and wishes her
Endless happiness.
MACBETH:
That's good. We didn't have much time to prepare.
The party would have been even more grand.
BANQUO:
Everything is fine.
I had a dream about the three Weird Sisters.
They told you some truths.
MACBETH:
I haven't thought about them.
But, when we have some spare time,
We can talk about that.
BANQUO:
Whenever you're free.
MACBETH:
If you join my plan, when it's time,
It will bring you honor.
BANQUO:
Only if I won't lose anything
In trying to increase it and can still maintain it.
My heart is free, and I swear my clear loyalty.
I will follow your advice.
MACBETH:
Rest well!
BANQUO:

Same to you sir.

Banquo and Fleance exit.

MACBETH *[To Servant]*:
Tell your lady to ring the bell when my drink is ready.
Off to bed with you.

Servant exits.

[Aside.]
Is that a dagger I see in front of me,
With the handle pointed my way?
Can I grab hold of you?
I can't touch you but I can still see you.
Are you an illusion, touchable yet invisible?
Or are you just a mind game,
An anxious thought from my tired mind?
I see you, as clear as if this were the real dagger
I hold in my hand right now.
You're leading me to the same destination I was headed,
With a similar tool in hand.
You trick my eyes, making their senses seem fake,
Or all-powerful.
I still see the dagger, and on the blade,
There are blobs of blood.
But I know that's not true.
It's my fearful conscious that paints
This bloody picture for my eyes.
Half of the world is in the dark sleep,
Fooled by nightmares while they rest.
Howling wolves creeps with quiet steps.
I don't want the stones to tell tales of my whereabouts
By echoing my steps,. It makes me terrified.
This is the moment for action. While I wait, he's alive.
Words are a poor substitute for action.

A bell rings.

I must go, the deed is done. The bell calls me.
Duncan, don't hear it, because it's a death knell
That's calling you to heaven or to hell.

Exit.

SCENE II. THE SAME

24 *[ENTER LADY MACBETH.]*

LADY MACBETH:

What has made them drunk, has made me brave.

What has put them to sleep, has fired me up. --Listen! --Quiet!

It was the shriek of an owl! He must be doing it now.

The doors are open and the sleepy guards are snoring.

I've drugged their drinks,

So that life and death are struggling over them.

MACBETH:

[From inside.] Who's there? --What's happening?

LADY MACBETH:

Oh! I'm scared they have woken up,

And it's not done. I'm worried that the plan will not go through.

--Listen! --I've kept their daggers ready so Macbeth won't miss them.

--If King Duncan hadn't looked like

My father when he slept, I would have done it myself.

--Is that you, my husband!?

Enter Macbeth.

MACBETH:

I've done what we planned.

--Didn't you hear a sound?

LADY MACBETH:

I heard the owl shriek.

Didn't you say something?

MACBETH:

When?

LADY MACBETH:

Just now.

MACBETH:

As I was going downstairs?

LADY MACBETH:

Yes.

MACBETH:

Listen! --Who's sleeping in the second room?

LADY MACBETH:

Donalbain.

MACBETH:

This does not look good.

Looking at his hands.

LADY MACBETH:

It's silly to call it a bad sight.

MACBETH:

One of them was laughing in sleep, and one said, "Murder!"

They woke each other up: I stood and heard them.

But they said their prayers, and then

Went back to sleep.

LADY SHACBETH:

Two of them were sleeping together in a single room.

MACBETH:

25   One of them said, "God bless us!" and the other said, "Amen,"

38

Because they saw me with these executioner's hands.
Hearing their fear, I couldn't even say "Amen,"
When they were saying, "God bless us."
LADY MACBETH:
Don't take it so seriously.
MACBETH:
But why couldn't I say "Amen"?
I really needed a blessing, but "Amen"
Got stuck in my throat.
LADY MACBETH:
We can't think about
What we've done or we'll go crazy.
MACBETH:
I thought I heard a voice say, "Sleep no more!
Macbeth has killed sleep"—the innocent sleep.
It stops our daily worries and gives relief from hard work.
Its heals hurt minds and is the most important part of life's meal.
LADY MACBETH:
What are you talking about?
MACBETH:
Again it said, "Sleep no more!" throughout the house!
"Macbeth has killed sleep, so now Macbeth
Will sleep no more. Macbeth shall never sleep again!"
LADY MACBETH:
Who said that? Remember, my worthy lord,
You're letting your thoughts get the best of you.
Go get some water and wash your hands clean.
Oh! Why did you bring these daggers from his room?
They should be left there. Go back and cover
The sleeping guards with blood.
MACBETH:
I can't go back.
I'm too scared to think of what I've done.
I can't bear to look at it again.

LADY MACBETH:
What a wimp!
Give me the daggers.
They dead can't hurt you.
If Duncan still bleeds,
I'll put it on the sleeping guards' faces bloody,
So it looks like they're guilty.

Exit. Knocking heard.

MACBETH:

Where is that knocking coming from?
Why does every sound scare me so much?
What are these hands? Oh, they could rip out my eyes!
Can all the water in the big ocean wash this blood
Off my hand? No, my hand would rather
Turn the whole big ocean red,
Making the green water red.

Enter Lady Macbeth.

LADY MACBETH:
My hands are as bloody as yours, but I'm embarrassed
To act like a wimp. *[Knocking heard.]* I hear knocking
At the back door. Quick! Let's go to our bedroom.
A little water washes away this crime.
How easy it is then! Your bravery
Has left you alone.—*[Knocking heard.]* Listen, more knocking.
Put on your nightgown, in case someone sees us
And thinks we are still awake. Don't get
So lost in your worrying.
MACBETH:
It's best if I don't know what I've done. *[Knocking heard.]*
Wake up Duncan with your knocking! If only you could!

Exit.

SCENE III. THE SAME

 [Enter a Porter. Knocking within.]

PORTER:

Wow, that's some loud knocking! If I were the gatekeeper of Hell, I'd get pretty tired of turning this key. *[Knocking.]* Knock, knock, knock. Who's there, in the devil's name? Maybe a farmer who ended his life because he thought he'd get rich? Come inside! Make sure you carry some handkerchiefs! You're going to get sweaty. *[Knocking.]* Knock, knock! Who's there, in the other devil's name? Well, here's a liar who could balance his lies, using it for both good and bad, who did really horrible things hoping for something better, yet couldn't lie himself into heaven! Come on in, liar. *[Knocking.]* Knock, knock, knock! Who's there? Well, here's an English tailor who arrived here, for stealing from a French pair of pants: come inside, tailor; you can cook your goose here. *[Knocking.]* Knock, knock. Never a moment of peace! Who could you be?—But it's a bit chilly for hell in here. I won't pretend to be a devil's doorman any longer! I had considered welcoming folks from all types of jobs, who picked the easy path

41

leading to eternal punishment. *[Knocking.]* Just a moment, just a moment! Please, do think of the gatekeeper.

He opens the gate. Enter Macduff and Lennox.

MACDUFF:

Did you go to bed really late, friend,

That you woke up so late?

PORTER:

Honestly, sir, we were partying until the late hours. Alcohol, sir, kept us up.

MACDUFF:

Why is that?

PORTER:

Well, sir, strong drink leads to a flushed nose, sleep, and the need to use the bathroom. Also, it gives you energy, but also makes you quite tired at the same time. So, too much of drink can be seen as tricky. It motivates and stops you at the same time. It makes a person brave, and then cowardly.

MACDUFF:

I believe drink controlled you quite a bit last night.

PORTER:

Indeed, it did, sir, right to my face! But I managed to regain control.

MACDUFF:

Is your master awake?

Enter Macbeth.

Our knocking must have woken him. Here he comes.

LENNOX:

Good morning, noble sir!

MACBETH:

Good morning to you both!

MACDUFF:

Is the King awake, honorable lord?

MACBETH:

Not yet.

MACDUFF:

He had asked me to visit him early.

I'm almost late.

MACBETH:

I'll take you to him.

MACDUFF:

I know this is a reason for celebration for you,

But it's still a job.

MACBETH:

Work that we enjoy soothes the discomfort.

This is the door.

MACDUFF:

I will dare to knock.

Because that's my duty.

Exit Macduff.

LENNOX:

Is the King leaving today?

MACBETH:

He is. He had planned as much.

LENNOX:

The night has been chaotic. Where we slept,

Our chimneys collapsed, and, as they say,

We heard strange cries of death in the air,

A bird squawked and screeched all night.

Some say the earth rumbled.

MACBETH:

It was a rough night.

LENNOX:

I don't remember anything similar to it in my short life.

Here comes Macduff.

MACDUFF:

Oh, horror, horror, horror!

I can't even say what I've seen!

MACBETH and **LENNOX:**

What's wrong?
MACDUFF:
Horror, horror, horror!
An unthinkable murder has broken open
God's chosen one and stolen life!
MACBETH:
What do you say? The life?
LENNOX:
You mean the King?
MACDUFF:
Go into the room, and disrupt your sight
With a new horror. Don't ask me to disclose.
See, and then express yourselves.
MACBETH and **LENNOX** go off scene.
Wake up, wake up!—
Ring the emergency bell.—Murder and betrayal!
Banquo and Donalbain! Malcolm! awake!
Break free from this deep sleep
And look death in the face!
It is a catastrophe! Malcolm! Banquo!

A bell rings. Lady Macbeth comes in.

LADY MACBETH:
What's going on?
Tell me, speak!
MACDUFF:
Oh, kind lady,
It's not for you to hear what I have to share.
Repeating it into a woman's ear,
Would shatter her.

Enter Banquo.

Oh Banquo, Banquo!?
The king, our royal leader, has been killed!
LADY MACBETH:
Oh no, what a tragedy!

What, here in our own home?

BANQUO:

Such a cruel act could happen anywhere. —

Duff my friend, I beg you, please tell us it's not true.

Enter Macbeth and Lennox with Ross.

MACBETH:

If I had died just an hour before this awful event,

I would've lived a happy life.

Unfortunately, now nothing is worth it.

The best of life is gone.

Enter Malcolm and Donalbain.

DONALBAIN:

What's wrong?

MACBETH:

You're the ones in trouble, and you don't even know it.

The source of your life has been stopped.

MACDUFF:

Your royal father's been killed.

MALCOLM:

Oh, by who?

LENNOX:

It seems like the people who were guarding him did this.

Their hands and faces were all smeared with blood.

So were their daggers, which we found

Untouched on their pillows.

They were in a state of shock and disarray.

No one could trust their lives with them.

MACBETH:

Oh, I do regret telling you this.

In my rage, I killed them.

MACDUFF:

Why did you do that?

MACBETH:

Who can feel all the things I was feeling at the same time?

No one!
My passion in the moment overpowered my sense of reason.
There was Duncan,
His pale skin color mixed with his flowing golden blood.
And his deep wounds looked like a crack in nature,
Opening it up for wasteful destruction,
And there were the killers,
Drenched in the signs of their act, their daggers!
Their clothing was shockingly soaked with blood.
Who could hold back?
I loved Duncan and proved it then!

LADY MACBETH:

I feel faint. I need help, help!

MACDUFF:

Take care of the lady.

MALCOLM:

Why do we keep silent,
When we should be talking about this?

DONALBAIN:

What can we say when at any moment,
An attack from a hidden enemy might catch us?
Let's leave. We're not done crying yet.

MALCOLM:

Nor has our deep sadness
Got us moving yet.

BANQUO:

Care for the lady:—

Lady Macbeth is taken away.

And when we've taken care of each other,
We will meet and question this terrible thing
To better understand it. We are full of fear and doubt:
I stand with God's protection and from there
I fight against the hidden threat
Of betrayal and evil.

MACDUFF:

I will fight too.

ALL:

We all will.

MACBETH:

Let's prepare ourselves quickly,

And gather in the hall.

ALL:

Agreed.

Malcolm and Donalbain remain.

MALCOLM:

What will you do? Let's not join them.

Liars will fake their sadness. I'm going to England.

DONALBAIN:

I'll go to Ireland. Our separate paths

Will keep us both safer. Here where we are,

There are threats even in men's smiling faces.

MALCOLM:

Our safest bet is to get away. This isn't over, but let's quickly leave.

Let's move along. It's reasonable to escape

To rescue oneself when there's no compassion left in sight.

Exit.

SCENE IV. THE SAME. WITHOUT THE CASTLE

33   *[ENTER ROSS AND AN OLD MAN.]*

OLD MAN:

After seventy years,

I've seen many terrifying hours and strange happenings,

But this is the worst.

ROSS:

Ah, wise father,

The sky has seen what people have done and is angry.

Look, it's much darker outside that it should be.

Darkness buries the earth's face,

When sunlight should softly touch it.

OLD MAN:

It's unnatural.

Last week I saw a tiny owl kill a grand falcon.

ROSS:

Strange. The king's horses, beautiful and fast,

Broke out of their barn as if to start a fight with humans.

OLD MAN:

It's said they ate each other.

ROSS:

They did! It shocked my own eyes,

That witnessed it.

Here comes honorable Macduff.

Enter Macduff.

What's the world like, sir, now?

MACDUFF:

Can't you see?

ROSS:

Is it known who did this horrible act?

MACDUFF:

Those that Macbeth has already killed.

ROSS:

Oh, such a sad day!

For what good reason would they do that?

MACDUFF:

They were tricked.

Malcolm and Donalbain, the King's two sons,

MACDUFF:

They've run away which now makes them look guilty.

ROSS:

It all really goes against nature.

Well, now it's likely that Macbeth will become the king.

MACDUFF:

He's actually already been named.

He's gone to Scone to be crowned.

ROSS:

Where's Duncan's body?

MACDUFF:

It's been taken to Colmekill for burial.

ROSS:

Are you going to Scone for Macbeth's coronation?

MACDUFF:
No, cousin, I'm going home to Fife.
ROSS:
Well, I'll go to Scone.
MACDUFF:
I hope you see things done well there. Goodbye!
But I have a feeling our old ways will be more comfortable than our new ways!
ROSS:
Goodbye, father.
OLD MAN:
Blessings!

Exit.

ACT III

SCENE 1. FORRES. A ROOM IN THE PALACE

35 *[Enter Banquo.]*

BANQUO:
You have it all now.
King, Cawdor, Glamis,
Just as the witches said.
I worry that you did some bad things to get all of this though.
However, it all makes me wonder.
The witches said that your sons would not even be kings.
Instead, I would be the start of a line of many kings.
If what the Weird Women said about you could come true,
Couldn't their words also be true for me?
Maybe they could make me feel hopeful.
But enough-- I can't think about this anymore.
Enter Macbeth as King, Lady Macbeth as Queen; Lennox, Ross, Lords, and
Attendants.

MACBETH:
Look, our special guest is here.

LADY MACBETH:

If he had been left out,

It would have been like a gap in our big party.

MACBETH:

Tonight, we're having a feast, Sir. I'd like for you to come.

BANQUO:

Your Highness, I'm always ready to do what you want.

MACBETH:

Are you going horseback riding this afternoon?

BANQUO:

Yes, my good lord.

MACBETH:

It would have been nice

If we could have had your good advice in our meeting today.

But we can talk tomorrow instead.

Are you going to ride far?

BANQUO:

I'll ride as much as it takes to fill the time until dinner.

And if my horse doesn't tire out,

I might borrow some of the night for an hour or two.

MACBETH:

Don't miss our party.

BANQUO:

My lord, I won't.

MACBETH:

We've heard that our guilty relatives

Have fled to England and Ireland.

They haven't admitted to their wicked killing of their father,

Instead, they're spreading strange stories everywhere.

But we'll talk about that tomorrow.

Get your horse ready.

Is Fleance going with you?

BANQUO:

Yes, my lord. It's time we got going.

MACBETH:
I hope your horses are fast and steady.

Banquo leaves.

Everyone may do as they please until the party begins.
I'll spend the rest of the day on my own
And get some rest. Until then, God be with you.

Lady Macbeth, the Lords, and others leave.

Hey, you, come here.
Are those men waiting for our orders?
SERVANT:
They are, my lord, just outside the palace gate.
MACBETH:
Bring them here.

Servant leaves.

Just being king isn't enough.
I need to be safe as well.
My fears about Banquo are increasing,
His noble nature makes him a threat.
He is brave and daring,
Yet he's very wise when it comes to keeping himself safe.
The only person I fear is him.
His strength and bravery make me feel small,
Just like Mark Antony felt in comparison to Caesar.
He bravely confronted the witches
The first time they called me king,
And told them to speak to him.
Then, like prophets,
They said he would be the father of many kings.
They put a crown on my head, but I don't have any children to
pass it to.
If all of this is true,
For Banquo's children I have ruined my thoughts!
For them, the kind Duncan have I killed!
Just for them!

All to somehow make them kings,
Banquo's children kings!
If this is the case, I challenge fate to a duel,
And ask it to fight me until I win!—Who's there?—

Enter a servant with two murderers.

Go to the door, and wait there until we call you back.

Exit Servant.

Was it not just yesterday we talked together?

FIRST MURDERER:

It was, my king.

MACBETH:

Well then, have you thought about what I told you?
In the past, it was Banquo who insisted on bothering you.
I didn't think of you as bad people.
I explained this to you in our last meeting.
The past is the fault of Banquo.

FIRST MURDERER:

You made it clear to us.

MACBETH:

I did so and I've more to say, which is the reason
For our second meeting. Are you so patient,
That you can let this go? Are you so saintly,
To let this man get away with all of this?
His past actions forced you into poverty.

FIRST MURDERER:

We are men, my king.

MACBETH:

Yes, in the category, you are considered men.
Just as hounds, and greyhounds, mixed-breed dogs, spaniels, and scrawny dogs, fluffy water dogs, and half-wolf dogs are all named dogs.
However, each one is a little different, and so it is the same with men.
Now, if you see yourselves in the list,

38

Not in the worst category of manhood, say so.
From there, I will tell you what needs to be done
And from there express my deepest thanks.
SECOND MURDERER:
I am one, my lord,
Who has lived a hard life. I'll do anything you want.
FIRST MURDERER:
And I another.
I'm so tired of troubles.
MACBETH:
The both of you understand Banquo was your enemy.
BOTH MURDERERS:
Yes, my lord.
MACBETH:
He is my enemy as well and he's so dangerous,
That every moment of his life threatens
My own wellbeing. Although I could
Easily use my power to get ride of him, I can't act that way.
People have expectations for me. That's why I need your help.
We must keep our plan hidden from others
For several important reasons.
SECOND MURDERER:
We will, my lord,
Do whatever you instruct us.
FIRST MURDERER:
Even risking our lives—
MACBETH:
Your dedication is clear. Within the next hour,
I'll tell you where to hide.
I'll share with you the perfect timing.
It has to be done tonight.
And to avoid any mistakes or flaws,
Fleance, Banquo's son, who is always with him,
Must die too. Prepare yourselves.

BOTH MURDERERS:
We are ready, my lord.
MACBETH:
I'll come to meet you soon... stay hidden.

Exit murderers.

The plan is set. Banquo, your soul's journey,
If it reaches heaven, must begin tonight.

Exit Macbeth.

SCENE II. THE SAME. ANOTHER ROOM IN THE PALACE

40 *[Enter Lady Macbeth and a Servant.]*

LADY MACBETH:

Has Banquo left the court?

SERVANT:

Yes, madam, but he will return tonight.

LADY MACBETH:

Tell the King, I would like to talk to him

When he is free for a few words.

SERVANT:

Madam, I'll do so.

Exit.

LADY MACBETH:

When we get what we want, but aren't happy,

It's safer to be the one who's hurt,

Than by causing harm, live in uncertain happiness.

Enter Macbeth.

What's happening, my lord, why are you alone,

Thinking only of sad thoughts,
Thinking of those things which should have been forgotten?
What's done is done, and can't be changed.
MACBETH:
We have only hurt the snake, not killed it.
This will come back to get us.
It would almost be better to be dead
Rather than eat our meals in fear and sleep in terror.
Duncan is in his grave!
After life's difficulties, he gets to sleep well.
Treason has done its worst.
Nothing can hurt him now.
LADY MACBETH:
Come on,
Gently, my lord, smooth over your worries.
Be happy and fun among your guests tonight.
MACBETH:
I will be, my love, and I hope you will be too.
Remember to look for and mention Banquo
Show him respect, with both your looks and words.
And remember, that while we entertain everyone,
We must hide our true feelings in these false smiles,
And make our faces masks to hide what we feel inside.
LADY MACBETH:
You must stop this.
MACBETH:
Oh, my mind is full of stings and worries, dear wife!
You know that Banquo, and his son Fleance, are still alive.
LADY MACBETH:
But they cannot live forever.
MACBETH:
That gives me hope. They can be defeated.
So, try to be happy. Before the night is over, something horrifying
will be done.

LADY MACBETH:
What are you going to do?
MACBETH:
I won't tell you, dearest one.
The light dims and the crow
Flies back to the shadowy woods.
You're surprised by my words: but stay calm!
Bad things, once started,
Often get stronger through wicked actions.
So, please, go with me.

They exit.

SCENE III. THE SAME. A PARK OR LAWN, WITH A GATE LEADING TO THE PALACE

    [THREE MURDERERS ENTER.]

FIRST MURDERER:

Who invited you to join us?

THIRD MURDERER:

Macbeth.

SECOND MURDERER:

We don't need to doubt him. He's given us
All the details of our mission,
And exactly how to execute it.

FIRST MURDERER:

Okay, we're in this together.
And our target is nearly here.

THIRD MURDERER:

Listen! I can hear horses.

BANQUO:

[From inside.] Can we get some light over here, please?

SECOND MURDERER:

That's him.

FIRST MURDERER:

His horses are moving around.

THIRD MURDERER:

They are within a mile.

That's the path from the palace gate.

> Banquo and Fleance enter with a torch.

SECOND MURDERER:

Light, over there!

THIRD MURDERER:

That's him.

FIRST MURDERER:

Get ready.

BANQUO:

It looks like it's going to rain tonight.

FIRST MURDERER:

Let it all come down!

> *Attacks Banquo.*

BANQUO:

Oh, betrayal!

> *Dies. Fleance escapes.*

THIRD MURDERER:

Who turned off the light?

FIRST MURDERER:

Did it get in the way?

THIRD MURDERER:

We only got one-- the son escaped.

SECOND MURDERER:

We lost half of our mission.

FIRST MURDERER:

We need to leave, and figure out what to do next.

43

> *Exit.*

SCENE IV. THE SAME. A ROOM OF STATE IN THE PALACE

[A feast is ready. Macbeth, Lady Macbeth, Ross, Lennox, Lords, and helpers enter.]

MACBETH:
Please sit down in your proper places.
You're all welcome here!

LORDS:
Thank you, your Majesty.

MACBETH:
I'll mix with the crowd and be a good host.
My wife is acting as the queen.
We'll ask for her greeting when the time is right.

LADY MACBETH:
Please tell everyone they are welcome. I feel it in my heart.

Enter the first murderer at the door.

MACBETH:
Look, they greet you with gratitude.
We're all equal here: I'll sit in the middle.

Let's be merry! Soon, we'll toast at the table.

--But you have blood on your face.

Approaching murderers.

MURDERER:

It is Banquo's blood.

MACBETH:

It's better on you than inside him. Is he gone?

MURDERER:

My lord, his throat is cut. I did that for him.

MACBETH:

You're the best of the killers!

MURDERER:

Kind sir, Fleance escaped.

MACBETH:

That brings back my fear!

Now I'm caged, trapped,

Held back by doubts and fears.

But is Banquo safe?

MURDERER:

Yes, my good lord. He's safe in a ditch with twenty deep slashes on his head.

A blow to nature.

MACBETH:

Thank you for that.

Now the grown snake is dead, but the tiny snake that got away.

His poison will grow over time.—Leave. Tomorrow we'll talk again.

Exit Murderer.

LADY MACBETH:

My dear husband,

You're not being very social.

Show your manners.

Banquo's ghost appears, and sits in Macbeth's place.

MACBETH:

What a pleasant surprise!—
Now, may we have good food and healthy appetites!
LENNOX:
Would you like to sit, your Highness?
MACBETH:
In this gathering, we have honored our country's heroes.
I wish Banquo was here. I'll scold him for being late!
I hope nothing awful has happened.
ROSS:
His absence, sir, only lets him down alone. If it pleases your Highness,
Would you honor us with your company at the dinner table?
MACBETH:
Well, I see the table's full.
LENNOX:
There's a place set aside right here, sir.
MACBETH:
Where? I don't see it.
LENNOX:
Over here, my good lord. What's troubling you, your Highness?
MACBETH *[seeing Banquo's ghost]*
Who did this?
LORDS:
What are you talking about, my good lord?
MACBETH *[speaking to Banquo's ghost]*
You can't accuse me! Don't look at me like that!
ROSS:
Everyone, stand up. It seems the king isn't feeling well.
LADY MACBETH:
Please sit, my valued friends. My husband often gets like this,
And has done since he was young. I ask you, stay seated!
His fit will be over soon.
He will be alright soon.
If you pay too much attention to him,

You might upset him and make this last longer.

Eat, and don't mind him.——Are you a man?

MACBETH:

Yes, and a brave one, who dares to face

Something which might even scare the devil.

LADY MACBETH:

Oh, really now!?

This is just like your usual fears.

Your imagination always gets away from you. Shame on you!

Why are you making such faces? When all's said and done,

You're just looking at a chair.

MACBETH:

Please, look over there!

Look! Don't you see it?

Why should I care?

If you can nod your head, you can speak too.——

If the dead must rise from their graves,

Then our graves will just be food for birds.

Ghost disappears.

LADY MACBETH:

What, have you lost all sense?

MACBETH:

If I'm standing here, I saw him.

LADY MACBETH:

For shame!

MACBETH:

Blood has been spilled before, even in the distant past,

Before laws were made to maintain peace.

Yes, and since then too, terrible crimes have happened

Too dreadful for the ears. There was a time when death meant

an end.

Now a man may rise again and push us from our seats.

This is even more strange!

LADY MACBETH:

My dear lord, your friends are missing you.
MACBETH:
I had forgotten.—
Don't stare at me, my most valued friends.
MACBETH:
I have a weird sickness,
But it's not a big deal to those who know me well.
Let's toast! Then I'll sit. Please, some wine for me.
I raise my glass to the joy of everyone at this table.
To our friend Banquo, I miss him.
I wish he were here.

Ghost appears again.

I cheer to him and to all! Here's to everyone!
LORDS:
We second that, and cheers to you.
MACBETH: *[seeing Banquo's ghost]*
Go away! Get out of my eyesight!
Go dig a hole and hide.
Your bones are hollow,
Your blood is cold, and your eyes are lifeless!
LADY MACBETH:
My friends, think of this odd behavior as simply a habit.
It's nothing more,
But it does ruin the fun a bit.
MACBETH:
I'm brave enough for anything!
But this vision will make me tremble like a baby!
Be gone, terrifying illusion! Go away!

Ghost disappears.

And with the ghost gone,
I'm a man once again. Please, stay seated.
LADY MACBETH:
You've disturbed our happy gathering with this chaos.
MACBETH:

Can such things happen and surprise us so suddenly?
It's odd to me to see you stay calm and keep
Your natural color, while my face turns white with fear.
ROSS:
What are you seeing, sir?
LADY MACBETH:
Please, don't talk. It just makes him worse.
We should call it a night.
And don't wait around, just leave.
LENNOX:
Good night and may better health
Come to our King!
LADY MACBETH:
Good night to everyone!

Everyone exits.

MACBETH.
"Blood will have blood," they say.
Stones have been known to move, and trees to talk
In an effort to reveal the secrets we keep.
--Has it gotten late?
LADY MACBETH:
It's almost morning.
MACBETH:
So, Macduff didn't show up
To our banquet?
LADY MACBETH:
Did you invite him, sir?
MACBETH:
I've heard some things whispered...
I've got spies everywhere.
Tomorrow, I'll go see the witches.
I need more information.
Even if it's bad,
I've gone so far into this that

There's no turning back.
I have plans which must be acted on.
LADY MACBETH:
You really need to sleep.
MACBETH:
Let's go to bed. My mind plays tricks on me
Because it's not used to the fear.
Yet, we've only just begun.

They exit.

SCENE V. THE HEATH

49 *[THUNDER. THE THREE WITCHES ENTER, MEETING HECATE.]*

FIRST WITCH:
What's wrong, Hecate? You look angry.
HECATE:
Do I not have a reason, old ladies as you are,
Rude and too daring? How did you dare
To trade and interact with Macbeth
In riddles and deadly matters?
And I, who is in charge of your magic,
The secret planner of all harms,
Was never invited to play my part,
Or show the greatness of our skill?
And, what's worse, all you've done
Has been but for a stubborn son,
Mean and angry!
Make things right now! Go away,
And at the bottom of a scary pit

Meet me in the morning: thither Macbeth
Will come to learn his fate.
Prepare your pots and your spells,
Your charms, and everything else.
I'll be in the air; I'll spend this night
To a gloomy and tragic end.
Big things must be done before noon.
On the edge of the moon
Hangs a large, misty drop.
I'll grab it before it hits the ground!
And that, purified by magic tricks,
Shall bring forth such unreal spirits,
That, led by the force of their illusion,
Will pull him into confusion.
He will deny fate, mock death, and place
His hopes above wisdom, kindness, and fear.
And you all know, overconfidence
Is the greatest enemy of humans.

      Music and song can be heard, "Come away, come away..."
Listen! I am called! My small spirit, look,
Sits in a misty cloud waiting for me.

         Exit.

50 **FIRST WITCH:**
Come on, let's hurry... she'll be back soon.

         They all leave.

SCENE VI. FORRES. A ROOM IN THE PALACE

    [ENTER LENNOX AND ANOTHER LORD.]

LENNOX:
> Such odd things have happened. The gracious Duncan
> Was pitied and loved by Macbeth. Brave Banquo was out too late.
> Perhaps Fleance killed him, since Fleance ran away.
> It seems nowadays people shouldn't walk out too late.
> How terrible it must have been for Malcolm and Donalbain
> When they murdered gracious father! Horrible act!
> Again, how it upset Macbeth! In his anger, he swiftly
> Tore apart the two wrongdoers who were drunk and asleep.
> Wasn't that good of him? And wise, too?
> After all, it would have upset anyone ro hear the guards deny it.
> So, I say, he has handled everything well. I think,
> If he had Duncan's sons jailed they would know
> What it's like to kill a father, and so would Fleance.
> Don't say a word though. I've heard because he missed
> The tyrant's feast, Macduff now has a target on his back.

Sir, do you know where he might be?
LORD:
The son of Duncan,
Whom the tyrant took the birth-right from,
Lives in the English court and King Edward
Welcomes him with grace. Macduff went there.
He's gone to ask the holy king for help and get allies.
So, hopefully with their help, we may once again have
Food on our tables, and peaceful nights sleep
Without having to worry about bloody knives at our feasts.
We miss those times. However, when Macbeth learned
Where Macduff had done, he started preparing for war.
LENNOX:
Did Macbeth send a messenger to Macduff?
LORD:
He did and Macduff refused to return.
Then the gloomy messenger turned around
As if to say, "You'll regret this.
He's not going to be please with this response."
He knew the king would not be satisifed.
LENNOX:
Well, maybe Macduff can be careful and keep distance.
He is like some holy angel to go all the way to the English court.
I wish for a quick blessing so he may
Save our country and help us get rid of this cruel leadership.
LORD:
I'll send my prayers with him.

Everyone exits.

ACT IV

SCENE 1. A DARK CAVE. IN THE MIDDLE, A CAULDRON BOILING

 [Thunder sounds. Enter the three witches.]

FIRST WITCH:
Three times the spotted cat has meowed.
SECOND WITCH:
Three times the hedgehog whined.
THIRD WITCH:
The monster screams:—'Tis time, 'tis time.
FIRST WITCH:
Circling the pot, off you go!
Into it, the poisoned guts let's throw.—
Toad, that under a cold rock
You boil first in this enchanted pot!
ALL:
Double, double, toil and trouble!
Fire, burn, and cauldron, bubble!
SECOND WITCH:
Slice of a swamp snake,

In the pot, boil and bake.
Eye of a newt, and a frog's foot,
Bat's hair, and dog's tongue,
Snake's fork, and the sting of a tiny snake,
Lizard's leg, and owl's wing,
For a strong trouble spell,
Like a wicked soup boil and bubble.
ALL:
Double, double, toil and trouble!
Fire, burn, and cauldron, bubble!
THIRD WITCH:
Dragon's scale, wolf's tooth,
Mummy of a witch, jaws and stomach
Of the hungry saltwater shark,
Root of a poisonous plant dug out in the dark,
Liver of a person who speaks evil,
Gall of goat, and pieces of yew
Thinly cut during the moon's eclipse,
Nose of a Turkish man, and Tartar's lips,
Finger of a baby born too soon.
Make the mixture thick and heavy.
Fill the ingredients of our pot.
ALL:
Double, double, toil and trouble!
Fire, burn, and cauldron, bubble!
SECOND WITCH:
Cool it with a monkey's blood.
Then the spell is strong and set.

54 *Enter Hecate.*

HECATE:
Oh, job well done! I like your hard work,
And everyone will get a share of the profits.
Now sing around the cauldron,
Just like elves and fairies in a circle.

Bring magic to everything you put in.

> *Music and a song: "Black Spirits." Hecate leaves.*

SECOND WITCH:

I feel a tingling in my thumbs,
Something wicked is coming!
Unlock doors! Who's knocking?

> *Enter Macbeth.*

MACBETH:

What are you mysterious witches doing?

ALL:

A deed that can't be named.

MACBETH:

I beg you, answer me!
Even if you unleash the winds and let them battle
Against the churches, even if the foamy waves
Destroy and swallow up ships,
Even if this world absolutely falls apart...
Answer what I ask you!

FIRST WITCH:

Speak.

SECOND WITCH:

Ask.

THIRD WITCH:

We'll reply.

FIRST WITCH:

Tell us. Would you prefer to hear it from us,
Or from our leaders?

MACBETH:

Call them, let me see them.

FIRST WITCH:

Pour in the blood of a pig that has eaten
Her nine piglets. Add the sweat that's dripped
From a criminal's brow and throw it into the flame.

ALL:

Come, high or low!
Show yourself and what you can do!
   Thunder. A ghostly vision of a helmeted head rises from the cauldron.
55 **MACBETH:**
Tell me, mysterious power...
FIRST WITCH:
It knows what you're thinking!
Listen to its words, but don't interrupt!
APPARITION:
Macbeth! Macbeth! Macbeth! Be careful of Macduff!
Beware of this thane from Fife.

> *A ghost appears. It is a soldier's helmet.*

MACBETH:
Whatever you are, thanks for the advice.
You've understood my worries correctly.— But I need to know more.

> *The ghost disappears.*

FIRST WITCH:
They won't take orders. Here's another vision.
It is more powerful than the first one.
   Thunder. A ghost appears. It is a child covered in blood.
APPARITION:
Macbeth! Macbeth! Macbeth!
MACBETH:
If I had three ears, I'd listen to you.
APPARITION:
Be fierce and brave! Don't worry about the strength of man!
No one born of a woman will harm Macbeth.

> *The ghost disappears.*

MACBETH:
Then let Macduff live!
What reason do I have to be afraid of him?
Well, just to make sure nothing goes wrong,
I'll control my own fate. You won't survive, Macduff!

That will stop my fear and I can again sleep despite the thunder.

Thunder. A ghost appears. It is a child wearing a crown, with a tree branch in his hand.

What is this?

That shows up like the heir of a king?

It wears the symbol of kingship on his infant head!

ALL:

Listen, but do not respond.

APPARITION:

Be as brave as a lion, proud, and don't worry about those who wish you harm!

Macbeth will never be defeated.

Until Birnam Wood moves to Dunsinane Hill to attack.

The ghost disappears.

MACBETH:

That will never happen!

Who can force the forest, command the tree to…

Pull its roots from the ground and move?

These are good signs!

—But my heart

Pounds to know one thing. Tell me, if your power

Can reveal so much, will Banquo's sons ever

Rule in this kingdom?

ALL:

Don't seek to know any more!

MACBETH:

I need to know! If you don't tell me, I hope a curse falls on you!

Let me know. Oh no! Why is the cauldron sinking? What's that noise?

A sound.

FIRST WITCH:

Show!

SECOND WITCH:

Show!

THIRD WITCH:
Show!
ALL:
Show him the truth and break his heart!
Appear like shadows, and just as quickly depart!
A ghostly vision of eight kings appear, in order. The last king holds a
mirror in his hand. Banquo follows them.
MACBETH:
You're too much like the ghost of Banquo. Go away!
Your crown hurts my eyes! Every one of you looks the same!—
Wretched witches!
Why are you showing me this?—A fourth!—My eyes start wide!
What, will the line go on till the end of time?
Another one!—A seventh!—I can't bear to see any more:—
And yet, an eighth appears, who carries a mirror
That shows me mor and mroe and more! More kings!
Terrifying sight!—Now I see it's true.
The blood-splattered Banquo smiles at me
And points at them as his own.—What! Is this really happening?
FIRST WITCH:
Yes, sir, all of this is happening—but why
Does Macbeth stand there so stunned?—
Let's go, sisters, cheer up his spirits,
And show him the best of our delights.
I'll enchant the air to make a sound,
While you complete your silly dance.
We've done our jobs in welcoming him.
Music. The Witches dance and vanish.
MACBETH:
Where have they gone?—May this awful moment
Forever be a cursed day on the calendar!—
Come in here!
Enter Lennox.
LENNOX:

What are your needs, Your Grace?

MACBETH:

Did you see the witches?

LENNOX:

No, my lord.

MACBETH:

Did they not pass you?

LENNOX:

Indeed, they did not, my lord.

MACBETH:

I hope the air they travel on is cursed!

And cursed be all those who trust them!—I heard

The galloping of horses... who was it that passed?

LENNOX:

It's two or three, my lord, they bring you news.

Macduff has escaped to England.

MACBETH:

Fled to England!?

LENNOX:

Yes, my lord.

MACBETH:

Time, you are ahead of my fearful acts!

The rushed plan never works unless the action follows closely.

From this moment, whatever I think, I'll do immediately.

The castle of Macduff I will surprise attack!

His wife, his children, and all unlucky souls

That follow him in his family line will be no more.

No bragging like a fool!

This act I'll carry out before my plan cools!

But no more visions!—Where are these gentlemen?

Come, lead me to them.

Exit.

SCENE 11. FIFE. A ROOM IN MACDUFF'S CASTLE

 [Enter Lady Macduff, her Son, and Ross.]

LADY MACDUFF:

Why did my husband flee the country?

ROSS:

You need to be patient, ma'am.

LADY MACDUFF:

He wasn't patient!

His running away was senseless!

ROSS:

You don't know if it was his wisdom or his fear.

LADY MACDUFF:

Wisdom! Leaving his wife, leaving his kids,

His home, and his titles, in a place

From where he runs away? He doesn't love us.

He lacks compassion. Even a tiny bird will stay,

Protecting her babies in her nest, against the owl.

All is fear, and there is no love.

And there's very little wisdom in him running away.

ROSS:

My dear cousin, stay calm. As for your husband,

He is noble, smart, thoughtful, and knows best

What suits the times best. I dare not say more.

I fear rumors as we drift on a wild and stormy sea

In all directions. —I must leave you now.

I won't be long until I come back.

Things will either get no worse or they'll get better,

Like they were before—my lovely little cousin,

Blessings on you, too!

LADY MACDUFF:

He has a father, and yet he's fatherless.

ROSS:

I'd be a fool to stay any longer,

I have to leave now.

Exit.

LADY MACDUFF:

My boy, your father is no more.

What will you do now? How will you survive?

SON:

Just as the birds do, mom.

LADY MACDUFF:

What, with worms and flies?

SON:

With whatever I can find, just like they do.

LADY MACDUFF:

Oh, my poor bird! You won't be scared of a net or a trap.

SON:

Why should I, mom?

Poor birds don't deserve to be hunted.

Despite what you say, my father isn't dead.

LADY MACDUFF:

Yes, he is gone. What will you do for a father?

SON:

But what will you do for a husband?

LADY MACDUFF:

Well, I can get plenty at any time.

SON:

Then you'll get them just to let them go again.

LADY MACDUFF:

You're speaking with all the cleverness you have!

SON:

Was Dad a traitor, Mom?

LADY MACDUFF:

Yes, he was to some extent, my boy.

SON:

What's a traitor, exactly?

LADY MACDUFF:

Well, someone who makes false promises and lies.

SON:

So does that mean that all liars are traitors?

LADY MACDUFF:

Every person who acts that way is a traitor
And must be punished.

SON:

Do all liars and swearers need to be punished?

LADY MACDUFF:

Every single one.

SON:

Who has to punish them?

LADY MACDUFF:

Well, the people who tell the truth.

SON:

Then all the liars and false swearers are silly
Because there are enough of them
To outnumber the truthful ones and punish them instead.

LADY MACDUFF:

Oh God, help you, my poor child!

But what will you do without a father?

SON:

If he were gone, you'd cry for him.

If you didn't, it would mean that I'd quickly have a new dad.

LADY MACDUFF:

Oh, you little chatterbox, you do talk a lot!

Now someone else enters.

MESSENGER:

Hello, kind lady! You do not know me,

but I respect your high position.

I think some trouble is coming your way.

If you would like some simple man's advice,

Don't stay here. Leave, take your little ones with you.

I'm sorry to scare you like this.

To hurt you would be cruel,

Something too close to who you really are.

May the heavens protect you!

I can't stay any longer.

Exit.

LADY MACDUFF:

Where should I go?

I haven't done anything wrong. But I now remember,

I am in this real world, where doing wrong

Is sometimes welcomed. Doing good can be

Seen as a foolish risk! Why then, oh no,

Why am I using that womanly defense,

To say I haven't done anything wrong?

Wait-- what are these men doing here?

Murderers enter.

FIRST MURDERER:

Where is your husband?

LADY MACDUFF:

I hope, he's in no place so unholy

That people like you can find him.
FIRST MURDERER:
He's a traitor.
SON:
You're lying, you thug!
FIRST MURDERER:
What, you little one!

Stabs him.

Young traitor!
SON:
He has kiled me, mom!
Run, please!
He dies. Lady Macduff runs out, shouting "Help! Murder!" while being chased by the murderers.

SCENE III. ENGLAND. BEFORE THE KING'S PALACE

61 *[ENTER MALCOLM AND MACDUFF.]*

MALCOLM:

Let's look for a quiet, private place where we can cry.

MACDUFF:

Let's instead be like brave men and

Look to protect our broken country.

MALCOLM:

What I believe, I'll cry out.

What I know, I'll believe and what I can fix,

When I get the chance, I will.

MACDUFF:

The country is in serious trouble. I'm not dishonest.

MALCOLM:

But Macbeth is.

Even someone with a good, noble nature may step back

When given a big responsibility. I hope you will forgive me.

My thoughts can't change who you are.

Even angels remain bright, even though the brightest angel fell.
MACDUFF:
I've lost all hope in that case.
MALCOLM:
Well, I am doing a fair level of doubting.
Why did you leave your wife and child in such a vulnerable state?
They mean the most to you, do they not?
And without saying goodbye? — Please,
Don't let these suspicions harm you.
I ask for my own protection. You may be truly honest,
Even if I think differently.
MACDUFF:
Oh, bleed, bleed, poor country!
I can't stop the bad from happening!
Especially when a ruler lets it happen.
—I wish you well, Malcolm.
I could never be the bad person that you think—
Not even for all the lands the tyrant holds
And all the wealth of the East.
MALCOLM:
Don't be upset.
I don't fear you.
I think our country crumbles under everything that's happened.
It cries, it bleeds and each new day adds a wound.
I believe, though, there'd be people who'd stand up and help me.
Here, from kindly England, I've been offered help from thousands.
However, even when I overthrow or defeat the tyrant,
My poor country will face more problems than it had,
More pain, and more varied difficulties than ever before.
This will all be caused by the person who takes over.
MACDUFF:
Who will that be?
MALCOLM:

It is me. Trust me, I know in myself

And I have all kinds of wrongs within me.

When my true self is revealed,

Macbeth will look as clean as snow and the poor country

Will think of him as an innocent lamb, compared

To the endless harm in me.

MACDUFF:

Hell couldn't find a better rival for Macbeth. He's awful.

MALCOLM:

He is ruthless, greedy, dishonest, deceitful,

Quick to act, cruel, and totally sinful.

But there's no end, no limit, to my excesses.

For instance, I love women. I can never get enough.

All the boundaries in the world won't stop me.

It's better for Macbeth to be king than someone like me.

MACDUFF:

It's unwise to give in to every desire.

This the loss of the throne for many rulers.

However, you can find a way to enjoy your pleasures in great abundance.

You are king.

MALCOLM:

Well, by becoming king it will likely

Cause me to have really disordered emotions.

I expect that I will feel a lot more greedy.

I could see myself taking the nobles' lands from them.

I could take their valuables.

I'd only want more and more.

MACDUFF:

This greed sticks deeper and grows with a harmful influence.

Sure, it has been the downfall of our previous kings,

Yet do not fear Scotland has resources to meet your desires.

Again, whatever you want can be balanced.

You may have some bad qualities, but you have many good qualities too.

MALCOLM:

But what I am telling you is I possess no good qualities.

I don't have a sense of justice, truth, moderation, firmness,

Generosity, endurance, kindness, humility,

Devotion, patience, bravery, strength.

Instead, I am attracted to sin.

Indeed, if I had the power, I would put our country in chaos.

MACDUFF:

Oh, Scotland, Scotland!

MALCOLM:

If such an individual is deemed worthy to rule, say so!

I am as I have described.

MACDUFF:

Fit to rule?

No, not even worthy of life.—Oh, unhappy nation,

When will you experience your healthy days again?

The most noble king, the one most holy, was your father.

The queen who birthed you, was like an angel.

Farewell! The evils that you inflict upon yourself

Have driven me away from Scotland.—Oh my heart,

This is where hope ends!

MALCOLM:

Macduff, your noble dedication and loyalty

Has cleared my doubts about your visit. Cunning Macbeth

Has tried to win my trust through certain manipulations,

And so I'm no longer too trusting. However, it is God above

Who will judge between us! For even now

I direct myself under your guidance, and

Take back what I've said. In truth, I'm not like anything I've just
described.

I haven't been in any relationships, never have I broken an oath,

I've barely wanted what was already mine.

Never have I broken a promise. I take as much pleasure
In honesty as in life. My true self belongs to you and our strug-
gling nation:
Indeed, even before you arrived here,
Old General Siward, with ten thousand soldiers ready for
combat,
Was already on his way to come help our country.
Now we'll stand together, and hopefully our just cause
Will bring about results. Why are you quiet?
MACDUFF:
When things are both good and bad at the same time,
It's hard to come to terms with it all.

A Doctor enters.

MALCOLM:
Alright, we'll talk more later. Is the King emerging, I ask you?
DOCTOR:
Yes, sir. Some poor souls are waiting for his help.
Their illnesses go beyond science, but as soon as
He touches them, they immediately get better.
MALCOLM:
Thank you, doctor.

Doctor departs.

MACDUFF:
What sickness is he talking about?
MALCOLM:
It's called "the evil."
A truly miraculous healing ability that this good king possesses!
I have often seen him do this during my stay here in England.
He helps the severely ill people, those who are swollen
And ridden with sores. They look pitiful, beyond hope
Of any medical intervention, yet he heals them.
He places a golden medallion around their necks, they pray, and
heal.
In addition to this extraordinary ability,

He also has a divine gift of being able to see into the future.
And many blessings surround his royal seat,
That show him to be full of grace.

Enter Ross.

MACDUFF:

Look, who's coming this way?

MALCOLM:

A fellow Scotsman, but I don't recognize him.

MACDUFF:

My cousin. You're welcome here.

MALCOLM:

I recognize him now. Dear God, please remove
Whatever makes us strangers!

ROSS:

Indeed, sir.

MACDUFF:

Is Scotland in the same state as before?

ROSS:

Sadly, our poor country is in a terrible state.
The sighs, groans, and screams, that tear the sky,
Are expressed, but overlooked.
Sorrow fills the air and good people's lives
End before the flowers in their hats wilt.

MACDUFF:

So sad!

MALCOLM:

What's the latest news?

ROSS:

Every hour brings more and more sadness.

MACDUFF:

How is my wife?

ROSS:

She is well.

MACDUFF:

And all my children?
ROSS:
They are well too.
MACDUFF:
Has the tyrant disturbed them?
ROSS:
No, they were peaceful when I left them.
MACDUFF:
Don't keep anything from me. What's happening?
ROSS:
When I came here to share the news,
Which I've carried with a heavy heart, there was a rumor
Of many brave men that were on the move.
People have to do something. The tyrant is out of control.
This is the moment to find help.
Your presence in Scotland
Would ignite courage.
The country really needs it.
MALCOLM:
Let them feel comforted!
We are on our way there. Generous England has
Given us brave Siward and ten thousand soldiers.
There's no better or more experienced warrior
That the world has to offer.
ROSS:
If only I could respond
With equally hopeful news! But I have words
That should be shouted into the wilderness,
Where no one should have to hear them.
MACDUFF:
What do they concern?
The general situation? Or is it a sorrow
That belongs to a single person?
ROSS:

There's no honest person
That doesn't share some sorrow, though the core
Relates to you alone.
MACDUFF:
If it's about me,
Don't withhold it, tell me immediately.
ROSS:
Don't be mad at me for delivering the heaviest news
Your ears will ever hear.
MACDUFF:
What do you mean?
ROSS:
Your castle was attacked and your wife and children
Were killed.
MALCOLM:
Heavens have mercy!—
Give words to your sorrow. The sadness that stays silent
Weighs heavy on the heart, threatening to break it.
MACDUFF:
My children, too?
ROSS:
Wife, children, servants—everyone
That could be found.
MACDUFF:
And I was not there!
My wife is gone, too?
ROSS:
As I said.
MALCOLM:
Be comforted.
Revenge will help you feel better.
To heal this deep pain.
MACDUFF:
He does not have children.—All of my dear ones?

Did you say all?—Oh wicked villain!—All?

What, all of my beautiful babies and their mother?

In one cruel attack?

MALCOLM:

React like a man.

MACDUFF:

I will do so.

But I must also feel it as a man.

I can't help but remember the things that were,

That were most dear to me.—Did heaven watch,

And not defend them? I am to blame! Sinful Macduff!

They were all attacked because of me!

It wasn't for anything they did,

But for what *I* did! Now may they rest in peace!

MALCOLM:

Use this. Turn your sadness into anger.

Don't numb your heart, enrage it!

MACDUFF:

Oh, I could weep like a woman,

And boast like a coward!—But, kind heavens,

Hurry up and finalize everything; bring me face to face,

With this enemy of Scotland

And let him be within the reach of my sword; if he escapes,

May heaven forgive him too!

MALCOLM:

These are brave words indeed.

Come, let's go to the King. Our forces are ready!

Macbeth can be defeated. Try to stay hopeful.

The dark night can't hide the dawn forever.

Exit.

ACT V

SCENE 1. DUNSINANE. A ROOM IN THE CASTLE

 [A Doctor and a Gentlewoman enter the scene.]

DOCTOR:

I've watched with you for two nights, but haven't found any truth in what you've said. When was the last time she sleepwalked?

GENTLEWOMAN:

Since the King left, I've seen her get out of bed, put on her night-gown, unlock her cupboard, take out paper, fold it, write on it, read it, seal it, and then go back to bed. And all this time, she's asleep!

DOCTOR:

It's very strange that she can sleep and yet act like she's awake. In this sleepwalking, has she spoken?

GENTLEWOMAN:

Yes, but I won't repeat what she said.

DOCTOR:

You can tell me and you should.

GENTLEWOMAN:

I won't tell you or anyone else because I have no one to back up my story.

Lady Macbeth enters, holding a candle.

Look, here she comes! She's sleepwalking, for sure. Watch her. Stand back.

DOCTOR:

How did she get that candle?

GENTLEWOMAN:

It was by her side and she always has it. She demands that one be in her room.

DOCTOR.

You see! Her eyes are open.

GENTLEWOMAN:

Yes, but she's not really seeing anything.

DOCTOR:

What is she doing now? Look at her rubbing her hands.

GENTLEWOMAN:

It's actually very typical for her to pretend to wash her hands like this. I've seen her keep it up for about fifteen minutes.

LADY MACBETH:

Look, a stain is still here.

DOCTOR:

Listen, she's talking. I'm going to write down what she says to remember it better.

LADY MACBETH:

Be gone, cursed stain! Be gone, I say! One! two! Well, then it's time to do it. Darkness is scary! Shame on you, my lord, shame! A fighter, and scared? Why should we be afraid when no one can challenge us? But who would have thought the old man had so much blood in him?

DOCTOR:

Did you hear that?

LADY MACBETH:

The Thane of Fife had a wife. Where is she now? Will my hands never be clean? No more of that, my lord, no more! You ruin every-thing with your fear!

DOCTOR:

Listen, listen. You've heard things you shouldn't have.

GENTLEWOMAN:

I'm sure she's spoken things she shouldn't have. God only knows what she's seen and done.

LADY MACBETH:

The smell of blood is still here. No perfume can make my hand smell nice. Oh, oh, oh!

DOCTOR:

What a deep sigh! There's a heavy burden on her heart.

GENTLEWOMAN:

I wouldn't want such a troubled heart for all the world's wealth.

DOCTOR:

Well, well, well.

GENTLEWOMAN:

May God help her, sir.

DOCTOR:

This sickness is beyond what I can handle, but I've seen sleep-walkers live out peaceful, good lives.

LADY MACBETH:

LADY MACBETH:

Wash your hands, put on your nightgown. Don't look so scared.

I tell you yet again, Banquo's buried. He cannot rise from his grave.

DOCTOR:

Hear that?

LADY MACBETH:

To bed, to bed. There's knocking at the gate. Come, come, come, come, give me your hand. What's done cannot be undone. To bed, to bed, to bed.

Exit.

DOCTOR:

Is she going to bed now?

GENTLEWOMAN:

Right away.

DOCTOR:

There are bad rumors going around.

Unusual actions cause unusual problems.

Troubled minds often show their secrets in sleep.

She needs God more than a doctor now.

God, forgive us all! Look after her.

Remove anything that could cause her pain,

And continue to watch over her. Well, good night,

She has completely shocked me.

I have thoughts, but I dare not express them.

GENTLEWOMAN:

Good night, good doctor.

Exit.

SCENE 11. THE COUNTRY NEAR DUNSINANE

[Enter, with drum and colors Menteith, Caithness, Angus, Lennox and Soldiers.]

MENTEITH:

The English army is nearby, led by Malcolm,

His uncle Siward, and the noble Macduff.

They all have good reasons for why they want revenge.

Even the most scared men would be inspired to help them in battle.

ANGUS:

Near Birnam Wood is where we will meet them.

They're coming from that direction.

CAITHNESS:

Who can tell if Donalbain is with his brother?

LENNOX:

For sure, sir, he is not. I have a list

Of all the important people.

MENTEITH:

What is the tyrant doing?
CAITHNESS:
He's at Dunsinane Castle.
Some say he's crazy and others, who hate him less,
Call it brave insanity.
He is definitely out of control.
ANGUS:
Now he feels his secret killings biting at his conscience.
Now, every minute, rebellions accuse him of betrayal.
Those he commands obey only out of fear,
Not out of love. Now he feels his title as king
Unsteadily hanging upon him, like a giant's robe
On a tiny thief.
MENTEITH:
Who can blame him?
When his troubled thoughts
Probably cause him much grief on the inside.
CAITHNESS:
Alright, let's march!
We need to show respect where it's truly owed.
Let's meet to cure our sick kingdom.
And with each of our steps, we aim to cleanse our country.
LENNOX:
Or do as much as it takes
To water the royal flower, and destroy the destructive weeds.
Let's start our journey towards Birnam.

They all exit, marching.

SCENE III. DUNSINANE. A ROOM IN THE CASTLE

 [Enter Macbeth, Doctor, and Attendants.]

MACBETH:
Don't bring me any more news. Let all of them go away!
Until Birnam Forest moves to Dunsinane,
I can't be filled with fear. What about young Malcolm?
Wasn't he born from a woman like everyone else?
The supernatural forces have told me this:
"Don't worry Macbeth! No one born of a woman
Will ever have control over you!" So go on, traitors!
Mix with the English!
I will never bend with doubt or shake with fear.

Enter Servant.

Curse you, you pale fool!
Why do you have that scared face on?
SERVANT:
There are ten thousand sss—
MACBETH:

'Geese,' you fool?

SERVANT:

No, soldiers, sir.

MACBETH:

You weak boy. What soldiers, clumsy boy?

Your pale face is telling me you're scared.

What "soldiers?"

SERVANT:

The English troops, sir.

MACBETH:

Get out of my sight!

Servant exits.

Seyton!— My heart feels heavy,

When I see— Seyton, I mean it!—This fight

Will either cheer me up or defeat me for good.

I've lived long enough and my way of life is fading.

All those things that should come with old age,

Like respect, love, obedience, plenty of friends,

I shouldn't expect to have, but instead, will suffer

Deep curses, insincere praise, breath,

75　The heart wants to deny this, but it can't. Seyton!

Seyton enters.

SEYTON:

What would you like, sir?

MACBETH:

What other news do you have?

SEYTON:

Everything you've been told is true, sir.

MACBETH:

I'll fight until my flesh is cut from my bones.

Hand me my armour.

SEYTON:

You don't need it yet.

MACBETH:

I'll put it on anyway.
Send out more horses, look all around the countryside.
Punish those who speak of fear. Give me my armor!
How is your patient doing, doctor?
DOCTOR:
She's not physically ill, sir.
Instead, her troubled thoughts keep her from resting.
MACBETH:
Cure her of that!
Can't you treat a sick mind,
Erase a deep-seated sorrow from the memory,
Erase the mental distress,
And with some kind of helpful medicine
Cleanse her overburdened heart of the dangerous
Thoughts that weigh it down?
DOCTOR:
For that, sir, the patient
Must help herself.
MACBETH:
Then forget useless medicine! I'll have none of it.
Come, put on my armour. Hand me my weapon:
Seyton, get going.—Doctor, my nobles are deserting me.—
Come, get ready quickly. If you could, doctor, discover
The disease in my kingdom and cleanse it,
I would applaud you so much that the echo would applaud you
right back.—Take it off, I insist.—
What strong medicine could drive out these English troops?
Have you heard anything?
DOCTOR:
Yes, sir. Your preparations for battle
Tell us to stay alert.
MACBETH:
Follow me with it.

76

I will not fear death or trouble until Birnam forest comes to Dunsinane.

Everyone leaves except the Doctor.

DOCTOR:
If I were far from Dunsinane,
It would be hard to convince me to return.

Doctor leaves.

SCENE IV. THE COUNTRYSIDE NEAR DUNSINANE. A FOREST IN VIEW.

MALCOLM:

Cousins, hopefully we can be safe soon.

MENTEITH:

Agreed.

SIWARD:

What forest is this before us?

MENTEITH:

Birnam Forest.

MALCOLM:

Let every soldier cut down a tree branch and hold it in front of him.

Then Macbeth won't be able to tell how many of us there are.

SOLDIERS:

We'll do it.

SIWARD:

We know he's waiting in Dunsinane for us.

MALCOLM:
He hopes to be successful,
But I have heard his soldiers are not loyal to him.
MACDUFF:
Let's not judge before we get there.
SIWARD:
The time is now.
We shall find out soon what's to come of this.
We know for certain that we must fight.
So, let's advance to war.

SCENE V. DUNSINANE. WITHIN THE CASTLE.

 [Enter Macbeth, Seyton, and Soldiers, following the rhythm of drums and flags.]

MACBETH:
Hang our flags on the castle walls!
The shout is, "They're coming!" The strength of our castle
Will turn their attack into a joke. Let them wait
Until hunger and sickness make them weaker.
If they weren't supported by those who should be on our side,
We could have bravely met them face-to-face,
And sent them back home defeated.

A scream of women is heard.

What's that noise?

SEYTON:
It is the scream of women, my lord.

He leaves.

MACBETH:
I have almost forgotten what fear feels like.

There was a time when a scream would have made me jump
And my hair stand on end. I've had my fill of horrors.
Even terrible things, that I think of often,
Cannot surprise me now.

Enter Seyton.

Why was there a scream?
SEYTON:
The Queen, my lord, is dead.
MACBETH:
She should have died later.
There would have been a better time for such news.
Tomorrow, and tomorrow, and tomorrow,
Crawls at such a slow pace from day to day,
Until the last moment of recorded time
And all our past days have guided fools
The way to a dusty death. Out, out, fleeting light!
Life is nothing more than a fleeting shadow, a poor actor,
That paces and worries his hour upon the stage,
And then is heard no more. Life is a tale
Told by an idiot, full of noise and anger,
Signifying nothing.

Enter a Messenger.

Go ahead and tell your tale.
MESSENGER:
My kind lord, I don't know how to explain it.
MACBETH:
Well, speak up, sir.
MESSENGER:
As I stood watching from Dunsinane hill,
I looked towards Birnam Wood. Suddenly, I thought,
The forest seemed to move.
MACBETH:
Liar!
MESSENGER:

Let me suffer your anger, if it's not true.

You can see it for yourself within three miles.

I declare, moving trees. Come look.

MACBETH:

If you lie, you'll be hanged from the next tree.

If your words are true, I don't care if you do the same for me.—

Now, I am unsure. I start

To question the tricky words of the devil,

Whose lies seem so realistic. "Do not fear, until Birnam's trees

Come to Dunsinane;" and now a forest

Marches towards Dunsinane.—Prepare for battle, out!—

If what he tells turns out to be true,

There's no point in running away nor in staying here.

Oh, I am starting to hate the sun and feel the world is undone.—

Ring the warning bell!—Blow, wind! Bring on destruction!

At least we'll die with our armor on our back.

Exit.

SCENE VI. THE SAME. A PLAIN IN FRONT OF THE CASTLE.

[Enter, with drum and flags, Malcolm, old Siward, Macduff and their army, carrying tree branches in front of them.]

MALCOLM:

We're close enough now. Drop your leafy branches,

And show yourselves for who you are.—You, honorable uncle,

Together with my cousin, your brave son,

Will lead our first fight. Noble Macduff and I

Will take over what else remains to be done,

Following our plan.

SIWARD:

Good luck to you.—

If we can find the tyrant's power tonight,

We deserve to lose.

MACDUFF:

Let all our trumpets sound! Give them full blast,

Those loud signals of danger and death.

Everyone exits.

SCENE VII. THE SAME. ANOTHER PART OF THE PLAIN.

 [ALARMS SOUND. ENTER MACBETH.]

MACBETH:
I'm tied to a stake. I can't escape,
But, like a bear, I must fight. —Who's he
Who was not born out of a woman? Such a person
Am I supposed to be afraid or not?

Enter Young Siward.

YOUNG SIWARD:
What's your name?
MACBETH:
You'll be scared to hear it.
YOUNG SIWARD:
No! Even if you call yourself a scarier name
Than any in hell.
MACBETH:
My name is Macbeth.
YOUNG SIWARD:

The devil himself couldn't say a name

More ugly to my ears.

MACBETH:

No, nor more terrifying.

YOUNG SIWARD:

You're lying, tyrant. With my sword

I'll prove the lie you're telling.

They fight. Young Siward is killed.

MACBETH:

You were born from a woman.

Weapons I laugh at,

Especially when held by a man born from a woman.

He exits. Alarms sound. Enter Macduff.

MACDUFF:

That's where the noise is.—Tyrant, show your face!

If you're killed and it's not by me,

The ghosts of my wife and children will still haunt me.

I can't attack helpless soldiers, whose duty

Is only to carry their staves. Either you, Macbeth,

Or else my sword, with an unblemished edge,

I will put away without using. That's where you should be;

By this great noise, some important person

Seems to be discussed. Let me find him, luck!

And I ask for nothing more.

He exits. Alarms. Enter Malcolm and Old Siward.

SIWARD:

This way, my lord —the castle's surrender is being handled gently.

People are no longer supporting the cruel ruler.

The day seems mostly to be yours.

There is little left to be done.

MALCOLM:

We have encountered enemies

That are striking close to us.
SIWARD:
Go ahead, sir, into the castle.

Exit. Alarms continue.

SCENE VIII. THE SAME. ANOTHER PART OF THE FIELD.

 [ENTER MACBETH.]

MACBETH:
Why should I play the silly game, and die
On my own sword?
These wounds will look better on them!

Enter Macduff.

MACDUFF:
Turn around, evil one, turn!

MACBETH:
I have avoided everyone else but you!
But go back! My soul has seen too much
Of your blood already.

MACDUFF:
I have no words for that comment.
My voice is in my sword.

They fight.

MACBETH:

You waste your time.

I live a protected life, which cannot be ended

By anyone born of a woman.

MACDUFF:

Well then, give up your false sense of safety now.

Macduff was not born in the normal way,

But was taken early from his mother's womb.

MACBETH:

Cursed is the person who tells me this,

It frightens me!

And these tricky devils can't be trusted,

They tell us one thing and mean another!

They promise us something and then take it away!

I won't fight with you.

MACDUFF:

Then surrender, you coward,

And live to be a spectacle for all to see.

We'll have your image, as we do of rare monsters,

Painted and displayed,

"Here is the tyrant."

MACBETH:

I will not surrender,

Or bow before young Malcolm!

And to be mocked by the crowd's curse.

Even if Birnam wood comes to Dunsinane,

And you stand against me,

Not being born of a woman,

I will fight to the end!

Attack then, Macduff!

They exit fighting. Alarms sound. Everyone retreats. Enter Malcolm, old Siward, Ross, Thanes and Soldiers, with drums and flags.

MALCOLM:

I wish the friends we're missing were safe.

SIWARD:

Judging by what I see, this great day was almost easy.
MALCOLM:
Macduff is missing, and so is your brave son.
ROSS:
Your son has paid the price of a soldier's life.
In the fierce battle where he fought, he died.
SIWARD:
He is dead, then?
FLEANCE:
Yes, and taken off the battlefield.
Your sorrow shouldn't be measured by his worth,
Because then it has no end.
SIWARD:
And he got his wounds in the battle?
ROSS:
Yes, on the front line.
SIWARD:
Well then, he truly was one of God's soldiers!
I would not wish for a better end for my many sons.
And so, it's time to mourn his death.
MALCOLM:
He deserves more sorrow,
And that's what I'll give him.
SIWARD:
There's no need for more.
They say he died well and paid his dues and so,
God be with him! Here comes comforting news.

Enter Macduff with Macbeth's head.

MACDUFF:
Greetings, King, for that is what you are.
Look, here is the cursed head of the tyrant!
We are free now!
We will combine our cheers in celebration!
Hail, King of Scotland!

ALL:

Hail, King of Scotland!

Celebration.

MALCOLM:

We won't much time to thank you for what you've done. We know you are tired.

My lords and relatives, you'll be called earls, the first ever in Scotland

To receive such an honor. What else needs to be done,

That suits the new times,—

Like welcoming back our friends who were exiled,

Who escaped from the grip of Macbeth and his wicked queen,

Who, it's believed, took her own life,

—this, and whatever else is needed

That demands our attention, with God's help,

We will do in the right way, at the right time, and in the right place.

So thank you to all, and to each one,

Whom we invite to see us at Scone for the crowning.

Cheerful celebration. They exit.